When she didn't get the surprises she wanted, Queen Loonia was so bad-tempered that all the servants fled from the castle in terror.

Soon, only little Billy Dingle was left. He had to do everything.

Nobody ever gave Billy a surprise.

Late one afternoon, while he was peeling the potatoes . . .
DISASTER STRUCK!

Queen Loonia hadn't been surprised for two whole days.
She flew into a tantrum.

"I want surprises right this minute! I shall give my most treasured possession to the person who brings me the biggest surprise!"

The next day, contestants from miles around arrived at the castle.
As Billy lowered the drawbridge, there was a mad scramble for the gate.

Henri Sweets presented his
Ice cream and Banana surprise.
"It is the most spectacular dessert I have
ever created," he said.

But then it melted all over the floor.
Queen Loonia was not impressed.

She locked him in the castle greenhouse
with her weird tropical plants.

Marvin Spark was sure his Explosive surprise would win.
"It is perfectly safe," he explained.

But when it blew up and frightened her pet dragons, Queen Loonia lost her temper and turned him into a frog.

James Gofaster took her for a spin through the royal forest in his Turbo Charged surprise.
"This is the fastest car in the land," he cried.

But on the way back, it broke down in a swamp.
Queen Loonia was furious, so she stormed off in a terrible mood and left
him there . . . with her crocodiles.

She really liked Dr. Slop's Monstrous surprise . . .
until it tried to kiss her.

"How dare you!" she shrieked, and chased them both out of the castle into the royal maze.

All day a large crowd gathered to see which surprise would win.
"All those surprises were rubbish," Queen Loonia finally announced.
"None of them will do."

The crowd began to tremble.
Then a small voice said, "Wait, I have a surprise."
"You, Billy Dingle!" said Queen Loonia.
"How dare you speak to me. Go and polish my submarines at once before I lock you in the tower. Anyway, you're just a poor boy from the village so what could you ever give me?"

The crowd fell silent.

Billy reached deep into his pocket and pulled out . . .

a tiny jar of multicolored Jelly Beans.
Queen Loonia stared at him in amazement. Then she jumped up from her throne with excitement, barely able to speak.

"How did you know?" she cried.
"Jelly Beans are my absolute favorite—especially the pink and yellow ones."

Queen Loonia kept her promise and gave Billy her
most treasured possession . . .

. . . Marmaduke, her pet killer whale.

Billy took Marmaduke home in his gold-plated
fish tank to meet his mom.

Meanwhile, Queen Loonia was in such a good mood that she threw a giant Jelly Bean party for everyone.

She had finally decided that the biggest surprises are not always the best.

First edition for the United States published 1992 by
Barron's Educational Series, Inc.

Text copyright © Richard Groves, 1992
Illustrations copyright © Mark Burgess, 1992

First published in the
United Kingdom by
J.M. Dent & Sons, Ltd

All inquiries should be addressed to:
Barron's Educational Series, Inc.
250 Wireless Boulevard
Hauppauge, New York 11788

International Standard Book No. 0–8120–4582–3

Library of Congress Catalog Card No. 91–13178

Library of Congress Cataloging-in-Publication Data

Groves, Richard.
   Surprise, surprise Queen Loonia/Richard Groves:
illustrated by Mark Burgess,—1st U.S. ed.
      p.   cm.
      Summary: A queen who likes surprises all the time
offers her most treasured possession to the person
who brings her the biggest surprise.
   ISBN 0–8120–4582–3
      [1. Kings, queens, rulers, etc.—Fiction. 2. Surprise
      —Fiction.]
I. Burgess. Mark. III. II. Title.
[PZ7.G9318Su 1991]
[E]—dc20
91–13178
Printed in Italy
234 987654321   CIP
                                                 AC

Surprise, Surprise Queen Loonia!

Richard Groves
Illustrated by Mark Burgess

BARRON'S

Queen Loonia only liked big surprises.
A private jet for her shopping, a roller coaster for the garden,
sixteen solid silver submarines for the castle moat — that sort of thing.